INTERRUPTING CHICKEN
AND THE ELEPHANT OF SURPRISE

INTERRUPTING CHICKEN AND THE ELEPHANT OF SURPRISE

David Ezra Stein

CANDLEWICK PRESS

It was after school for the little red chicken.

"Well, Chicken," said Papa, "did you have a good day at school?"

"Yes, Papa! And today my teacher told us every story has an elephant of surprise. So let's read a story, and we'll find the elephant."

"Chicken, she wasn't talking about an elephant. She was talking about an *element* of surprise."

"What's an element of surprise?"

"It's the part of the story that makes you say, 'Whoa!
I didn't know *that* was going to happen,'" said Papa.

"An elephant in a story always makes me say, 'Whoa!'
So please, let's read a story together."

"All right, fine. But I don't expect you'll find
any elephants in *this* story. . . ."

After a long, lonely winter in the cave, the Ugly Duckling was growing desperate. "I don't care if they tear me to pieces; I must be near those glorious creatures for just one moment," he said, as he flung himself toward the flock of swans.

To his amazement, the graceful birds did not attack or tease him, but seemed to accept him as one of their own. He peered into the water at his reflection, gasped, and said—

"Chicken! There are no elephants in *The Ugly Duckling*."

"Every good story has one. That's what my teacher said."

"That's ridiculous."

"Is *The Ugly Duckling* a good story?"

"Well, yes, but —"

"Then it must have an elephant of surprise.
Let's try another book."

Enchanted by Rapunzel's beautiful   singing, the prince drew near the tower. He had waited for this night. "Rapunzel, Rapunzel," he called, "let down your hair." Silently, a braid of Rapunzel's hair slid down the tower wall. "Come to me, my prince," called a melodious voice above. With all haste, the prince began to climb. When he reached Rapunzel, he gazed at his love, and she said,—

"Chicken, I *know* there is no elephant in *Rapunzel.*
That is just plain ludicrous."

"Don't you feel sorry for the elephant, Papa?
All alone, waiting for someone to find him.
Read another story and we'll find that poor elephant."

"Chicken, this is silly."

"It's my homework! Ms. Gizzard said to read three books and find the elephants in all of them."

"Okay," Papa sighed. "Here comes another story, with *no* elephants."

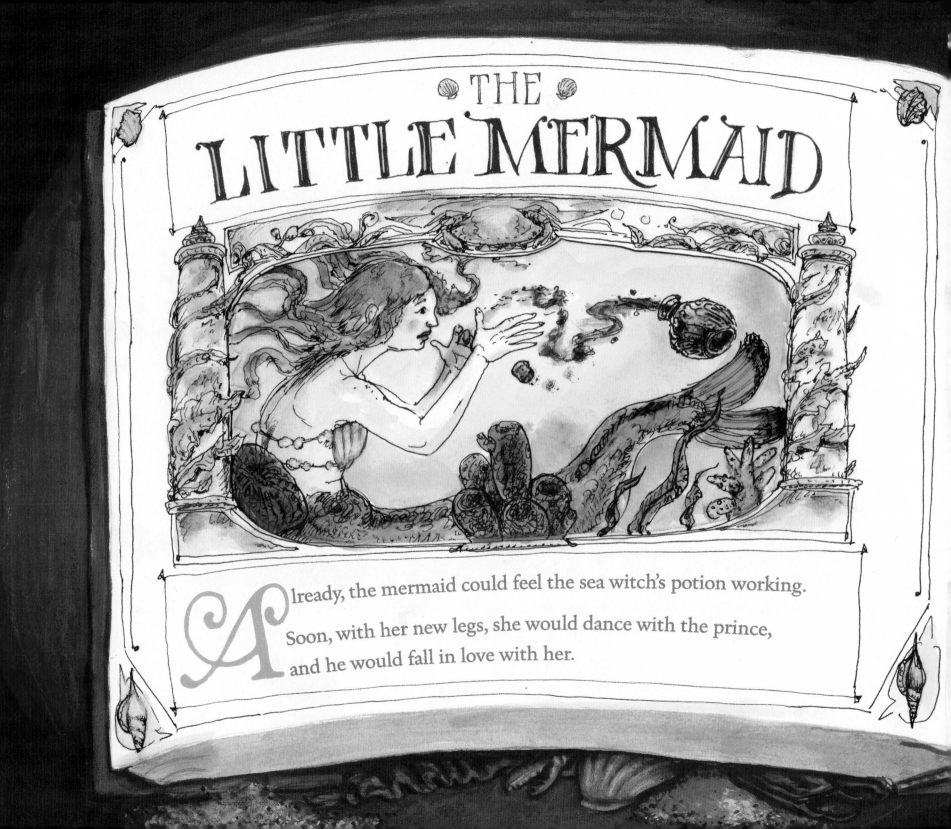

THE LITTLE MERMAID

Already, the mermaid could feel the sea witch's potion working.

Soon, with her new legs, she would dance with the prince,

and he would fall in love with her.

As she crawled out of the waves, a sharp pain passed through her. She fell to the steps of the palace, and knew only darkness.

When she awoke, the prince himself was standing over her. In the moonlight, she saw that her wish had come true. She finally did have legs—

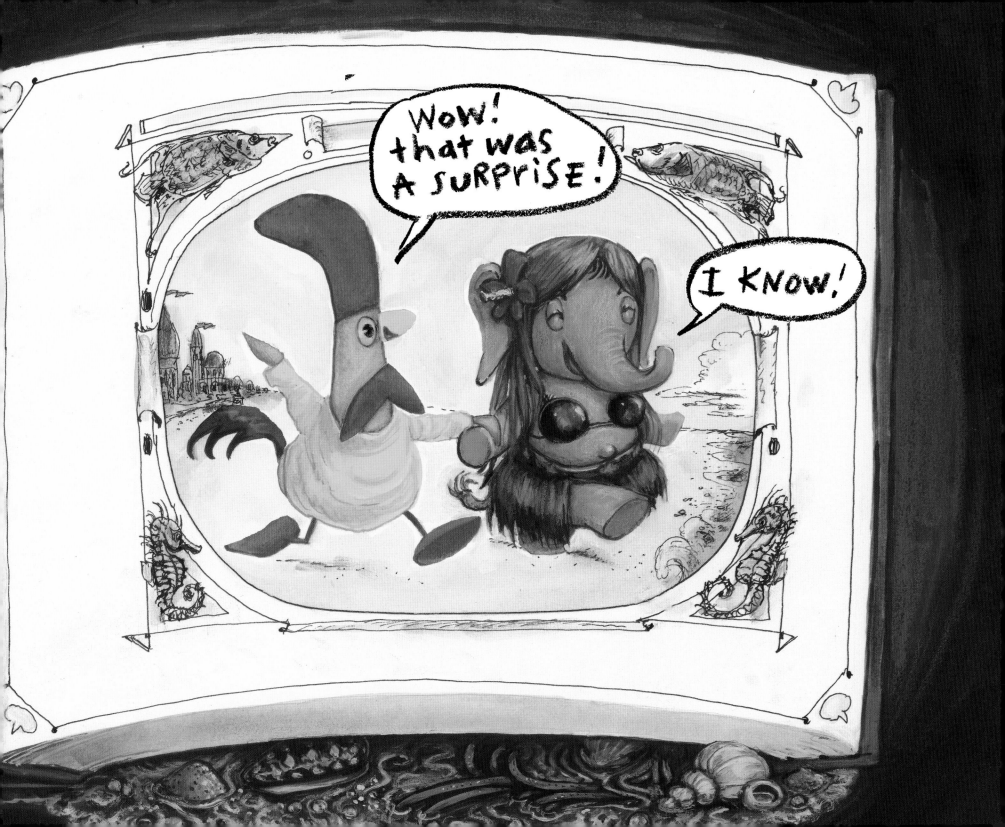

"Well, Chicken, are you happy? You've put an elephant in every story. But now I'm going to *tell* you a story and I'll make sure there are *no* elephants."

"Okay, Papa! And I'll draw the pictures."

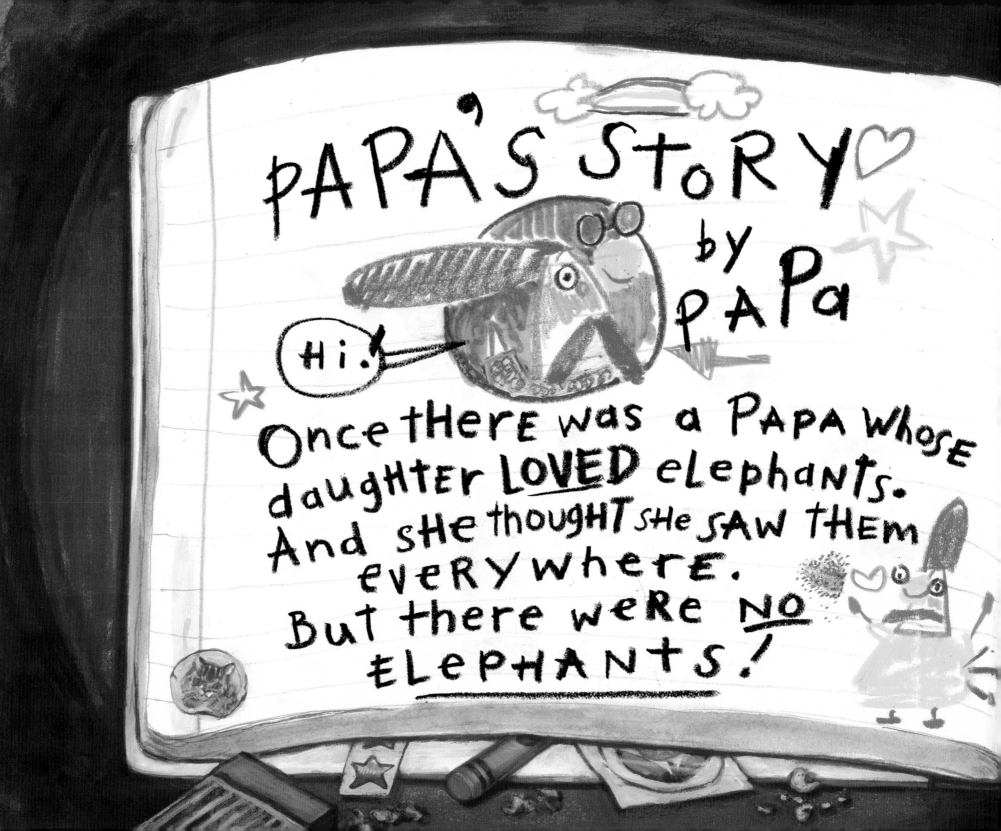

"Oh, Papa! I knew there'd be an elephant in the story."

"So did I, somehow," said Papa.

"And it was right at the end," said Chicken.
"What a great surprise!"

"Are we done, Chicken?"

"Yes, Papa."

"Now you can help me with my math homework!"

9/18
E
Stein

To Sam and Hannah:
you make every day a surprise

First edition 2018

Library of Congress Catalog Card Number pending

ISBN 978-0-7636-8842-4

18 19 20 21 22 23 CCP 10 9 8 7 6 5 4 3 2 1

Printed in Shenzhen, Guangdong, China

This book was typeset in Malonia Voigo.
The illustrations were done in watercolor, water-soluble crayon,
china marker, pen, opaque white ink, and tea.

Candlewick Press
99 Dover Street
Somerville, Massachusetts 02144

visit us at www.candlewick.com